THE EMPEROR'S NEW CLOTHES

**Published in Great Britain by World International Publishing Limited.
Great Ducie Street, Manchester M60 3BL.**

Copyright©MCMLXXXIII by Ottenheimer Publishers Inc.   All rights reserved. Printed in Finland.

SBN 7235 3873 5

THE EMPEROR'S NEW CLOTHES

Many long years ago, in a far distant land, there lived an Emperor who loved new clothes more than anything else in the whole world. He cared more for his beautiful clothes than for his people, his soldiers, or even his own family.

Soon there was to be a great feast day in the kingdom, and the Emperor thought only of the clothes he would wear. He decided that his clothes for the feast day would be the finest and most beautiful ever made. He said that he would pay anything for such clothes; in fact he offered gold and jewels and great treasure to the tailor who would make such fine clothes for him.

All the tailors in the land came to the Emperor's castle in the hope that they might be chosen to make the Emperor's new clothes.

One by one they went before the Emperor, showing their patterns and materials. The tailors brought velvets and laces, furs and gold threads; but still the Emperor was undecided. The Emperor said that he would decide within a week.

Near the end of the week the court jester brought two unknown tailors before the Emperor. They claimed that they would use special designs and materials to make the most unusual clothes in the world for the Emperor.

But, the two men were not tailors at all—they were swindlers who wanted to cheat the Emperor so that he would give them all his treasure.

The two men told the Emperor that they would weave for him the most beautiful and unusual cloth ever seen. They would make a suit of clothes from this material which would have a magical quality.

Only wise men who worked well would be able to see the clothes. To foolish men the clothes would seem to be invisible.

The Emperor was delighted to hear this—surely his clothes would be the most unusual in the whole world. He also knew that if his ministers could not see the clothes they were foolish men not suited for positions of authority. The Emperor decided that these men would make his new clothes and he installed them in a room in his castle to begin their work.

The Emperor, accompanied by his daughter and two of his ministers, visited the men. The swindlers were busy at an empty spinning wheel. The two ministers could not see anything but, not wanting to appear foolish, they exclaimed, "Oh, how fine. How beautiful!" The Emperor also saw nothing, but he exclaimed, "Magnificent! I can't wait for the clothes to be finished!"

The two swindlers pretended to weave the magical cloth, and every day they received more gold and jewels from the Emperor's treasure house. Every day the Emperor's ministers visited the swindlers to see how the work was progressing. Still they could not see the magical cloth but, not wanting to admit, this they reported that the cloth was the most beautiful in the world.

The feast day arrived and the two swindlers announced that the clothes were ready at last. The Emperor stood in his underwear as the swindlers pretended to fit the clothes they had pretended to make. They pretended to tie a sash around his waist and to place a cape around his shoulders. Then they stepped back. "How splendid you look!" the Emperor's ministers cried. "What beautiful clothes!"

"Perfect!" the Emperor said. "Now the procession may begin!" The Emperor's family and his ministers took their places for the procession. As the Emperor mounted his horse, the swindlers and the jester filled their pockets with the gold and treasure which the Emperor had given them. They ran through the town as fast as their legs would carry them, never to be seen in the kingdom again.

Thousands of people lined the streets; banners flew from every building as the procession began. The shops and schools were closed because everyone wanted to see the Emperor in his new clothes. The Emperor sat proudly on his horse, smiling and waving to the people. The people could not see any clothes, but they all nodded their approval, for none wanted to appear foolish in the Emperor's eyes.

A little boy stepped forward from the crowd. "The Emperor is wearing his underwear! He has no new clothes!" he shouted. "Pay no attention to the child," said his father. But many people had heard what the little boy had said, and one person whispered to another until everyone admitted that in actual fact the Emperor was not wearing any new clothes.

The Emperor had heard what the little boy had shouted, and he knew that it was true. He now understood that clothes were not the most important things in the world, for his vanity had cost him all his treasure of gold and jewels.